T0065250

2084

Bill Miller, Kevin O'Leary, and a Failed *Shark Tank* Episode

PAUL BOUCHARD

2084
BILL MILLER, KEVIN O'LEARY, AND A
FAILED *SHARK TANK* EPISODE

iUniverse books may be ordered through booksellers or by contacting:

iUniverse
1663 Liberty Drive
Bloomington, IN 47403
www.iuniverse.com
844-349-9409

ISBN: 978-1-6632-2541-2 (sc)
ISBN: 978-1-6632-2542-9 (e)

Library of Congress Control Number: 2021915844

Print information available on the last page.

iUniverse rev. date: 08/04/2021

For Ayn Rand, Mark Cuban, Kevin O'Leary, Steve Ballmer, Adam Andrzejewski, Mark Zuckerberg, Peter Schweizer, Peter Thiel, Jeff Bezos, and Elon Musk. Their ideas will shape the future.

Bureaucracy has an innate tendency to
expand and make work for itself.
(quoted from *The Economist*)

A DREAMY
IDEA IN 2020

WE WERE ON A CONVOY in southern Afghanistan, a dozen vehicles or so, and the sun was setting. Shorty looked at me—I was on his left—and he remarked just how nice the sunset was, the red-purple hue off the mountains. Then I remember a loud boom, and the next thing I knew, I was upside down, our Humvee flipped over. We were less than ten minutes from our destination when that IED went off. Thankfully, we weren't one of the ammo trucks because I wouldn't be here talking to you if that were the case.

I remember being in and out of consciousness as the medics worked on me and my battle buddies. We were all alive and accounted for, but we were all injured and hurting. I had this constant numb ringing sound in my head, and my back was killing me. When I was conscious, I felt some tingling in my lower legs.

I remember being placed on a gurney and loaded up on a chopper. The MASH station patched me up best they could, and then the four of us—Lieutenant Johnson, Sergeant Harris, PFC Alberto "Shorty" Gonzalez, and me—were flown to Germany for more medical attention.

A smiling female doctor placed the clear plastic mask over my mouth and nose. "This will make you sleep during the surgery," she told me. "Your TBI symptoms are steadily diminishing, which is good. We just need to fix your spine. You can expect a full recovery."

I fell asleep, but then the strangest thing happened: I actually felt myself floating out of my body, hovering above it. I could see the medical staff working on my back, placing me first to my side and then turning me completely so I was sleeping on my stomach.

It was surreal—literally an out-of-body experience—and then I remember meeting him, Mr. Wonderful, Kevin O'Leary.

Welcome.

Where am I?

You're here, in my wonderful place.

Is this heaven? The spirit world? Where are we?

I call it my place, the Wonderful Wonderland *pour moi,* Mr. Wonderful.

You're one of the Sharks on my favorite show, *Shark Tank.*

Right you are, grasshopper. And that's why you, Bill Miller, are here. I know you've got a business idea, and I want to hear it. But first, can I offer you anything to drink? Water, beer, wine—you know I'm partial to wine.

I guess I'll have a glass of wine. You're having a glass too, right?

But of course. Mr. Wonderful doesn't miss the opportunity to partake in the world's best beverage.

Knights 1 and 2, please pour us each a glass of wine.

Who are those two?

They are part of the Chevaliers de Tastevin, knights entrusted to protect some of the finest burgundy wines. I'm partial to burgundies you know. Whaddaya say we open up a bottle and have a few glasses?

Sounds like a plan.

I have just the perfect selection. A Joseph Drouhin Montrachet Grand Cru Marquis de LaGuiche. A 2017 vintage. Most excellent. Trust me.

Okay. I know so little about wines, but it sounds good. Sure, I'll have a glass.

Then again, we could go with my Kevin O'Leary Red Wines Gift, but I'm actually saving those particular bottles for my next run on QVC. And, good news, Sergeant Miller—I finally got my wine brand into two hundred Costco stores in the US. Did you know Costco is the largest seller of wines in the US, perhaps the entire world?

No, sir, I didn't know that.

Well, they are, and now you know.

Congratulations on obtaining Costco as a key distributor.

Thank you. *Merci.* Mr. Wonderful often gets his way.

In military terms, we say you accomplish the mission.

Exactly. I, Mr. Wonderful, accomplish the mission. Well, shall we? Knight 1, pour me a glass of the Joseph Drouhim Montrachet. Ah, yes … thank you, Knight 1. Now Knight 2, please do the same for my guest, Sergeant Bill Miller.

Cheers, my friend.

Cheers.

A votre sante, as the French say.

Yes, thank you.

Thank you, Knight 1. Now, Mr. Miller, please have a seat, and before you tell me about your intriguing investment opportunity, tell me about yourself and your family.

Sure. As you know, I'm Bill Miller. I'm twenty-four years old, and I'm from Lubbock, Texas. I'm a second-year law student at

Texas Tech Law School, pursuing a joint JD/MBA. Just about a year ago, my studies got interrupted because my National Guard unit got mobilized to do a tour in Afghanistan. I'm a truck refueler for the unit.

I see. Very well. Thank you for your service, young man. By the way, what do you think of the wine?

It's real good, Mr. Wonderful.

I'm glad you like it. Proceed.

Well, I have a sibling, my older brother, Mark. He works for a start-up in Austin, and he's a big part of my business idea. He works in data analytics.

Impressive.

Yeah, he's really smart. And I have great parents. My dad is a painting contractor—both residential and commercial—and my mom is an administrative assistant for the local hospital.

Very well. Nice family.

Thanks.

So you want to go on *Shark Tank* to pitch your business idea?

Absolutely. It's a dream of mine.

Well, Mr. Wonderful is here to help. First, tell me how you came up with your business idea.

Sure. It was a couple years back when I joined my local National Guard unit, and I began to notice stuff. For example, I had to fill out tons of paperwork to get paid, and I began to notice problems with my monthly pay. It took the headquarters agency in Austin five months to finally send me a paycheck. That's five drills without getting paid. And when I finally received a paycheck, there were errors in it too. Basically, they had my rank wrong, which messed up everything. It finally got all sorted out, but the process took close to another six months. Every month, my sergeant would tell me to fill out more paperwork, and we'd send it to Austin. It took forever to get things straightened out.

Then I started chitchatting with fellow members in my platoon. I noticed many of them also had problems with their pay. The light bulb really went off when I disputed an erroneous charge on my credit card, unrelated to the army, which involved the hacking that took place at some Target stores. I saw a charge for a purchase at Target that I never made, and I called the credit card company and explained the facts to them, and the whole thing was resolved in less than ten minutes. No paperwork to fill out. All done over the phone.

I thought, *Why can't the government be as efficient as Mastercard or Visa?* Also, one time, I watched a TV program—I think it was *60 Minutes*—about all the fraud that's going on with Medicare and the inefficiency at the VA. Estimates are that 10 percent of all Medicare payments are fraudulent, and still a larger percentage are wasteful. Then I researched the fraud rate with credit card companies like Mastercard. Their fraudulent billing is around 1 percent. As for the VA, *60 Minutes* also did a segment on them where their new director revealed the VA had six websites. He told his management team to have one official website ready in two months. I mean, how wasteful is it to have six websites? I realized if the government was run more like a business, the government would save the taxpayers a ton of money. See, I'm heavily influenced by my family. My dad runs his business real tight—he knows where every penny goes, and he has twenty employees. My mom works at the hospital, and she has all these stories about the waste and inefficiencies in billing and human resources there. Then I've got my brother who's in the hot field of data analytics, which brings efficiencies to the marketplace.

Well, young man, you've definitely identified a problem. Fair to say the problem is waste and fraud in government services?

Exactly, Mr. Wonderful. The army gives us annual ethics training where they really stress the point that government

5

employees—including military members—have a duty to report waste, fraud, and abuse.

Nice. I'm all ears. Tell Mr. Wonderful how you plan to fix this mess.

In a nutshell, Mr. Wonderful, my brother and I will start a company that will handle finance, payroll, travel services, and hiring for various government agencies. Our plan is to target federal agencies first, but eventually, we'll also target state and local government agencies. The waste in government is out of control. I have a lot more examples. Take travel, for example. The government sends so many employees, including military members, to conferences. Airline fares, hotels, and car rentals are all very expensive. Many of the conferences the government hosts or sends employees to can be done by video conference, which would save a lot of money. And when it comes time to book one's travel with the military, the online travel system, called DTS for Defense Travel System, is very cumbersome and complicated. It takes tons of time just to book travel. Contrast that to when I travel for personal reasons. I can book a flight, hotel, and car rental all in ten minutes, while through DTS, it will take me an hour or two, and then I have to wait for approval authorities, which also takes a lot of time. And then, DTS is all done through a government credit card, and so often, the government employee, including military members, has to pay the credit card bill without first being reimbursed by the government. Sometimes we get reimbursed on time, but quite often, we don't. We have to scan receipts and fax or email them over, and at times, we get error messages back. It's all a big mess. In our National Guard unit, we call DTS the Do Not Travel System. It's that inefficient.

That's funny, grasshopper. It's also sad. Mr. Wonderful is all about money and efficiency. I must inform you that I often ask prospective entrepreneurs about their customer-acquisition costs.

In your case, how are you going to get government agencies to agree to your payroll and travel and human resources services when they've got tons of government employees doing the work? You've identified inefficiencies in certain government services, but the problems you'll face are the many government workers who benefit from these services. It's their jobs, and nobody wants to lose their job. Plus, quite a few government employees are members of a union. Good pay, benefits, pensions. Sergeant Miller, Mr. Wonderful always speaks the truth. Your problem is not a market inefficiency problem, but a political one. Good luck fighting city hall, my friend.

You bring up good points, Mr. Wonderful, but I do have a plan that will not only bring better services, but also save money.

I'm listening.

In a word, transparency. Tell the people the facts. Especially tell the taxpayers what the cost comparisons are. With data analytics, we can do that.

Are you sure, grasshopper?

Yes. Absolutely. My brother, Mark, can figure out what the payroll, finance, travel, and human resources costs will be for our company, and with my legal background, I'll be continually filing Freedom of Information Act, "FOIA," requests. We, as taxpayers, have a right to know how much our government is spending on services. The government is already contracting out certain services to companies like Boeing and Microsoft and Booz Allen. We too want to submit bids for certain government services. Not satellites or aircraft, but human resources services like payroll, travel, and hiring. Our company will be called DPTM Corp. The acronym stands for Don't Pay Too Much. With my FOIA requests, and with my brother's analytical skills, we'll be able to figure out how many government workers work at a certain agency, what their salaries are, how much the government is paying to lease the building, costs like that. We think we'll be very competitive with our bids.

How?

By providing a motivated workforce who will work from home. We'll have state-of-the-art software, motivated customer service representatives, and we won't have all the overhead costs that come with commercial leases because our employees will work from their homes and apartments. And 401(k) plans are less expensive than defined-benefit pensions.

Young man, companies like Microsoft, Boeing, and Northrup Grumman are private companies that fill a need for a service that the government can't provide. But your business plan is to provide human resources services to government agencies, and the government agencies have tons of government employees providing those services. Good luck fighting the unions, my friend. Your business idea is a dog. It sucks, and it won't work. Mr. Wonderful speaks the truth.

I respectfully disagree, sir. With DPTM, we'll be able to show that the government is spending X to provide certain services, while we'll be able to provide those same services at X minus 20, 30, 40 percent. Do you know that Elon Musk's SpaceX can launch satellites into space via rockets at half the price that Boeing can?

Elon Musk is a genius, my friend. By the way, my son works at Tesla. You're smart, Sergeant Miller, but you're no Elon Musk.

I never claimed to be, sir. But my point is we will not only market ourselves as an efficient low-cost provider, but we will show the taxpayers how much money the government would save by awarding our company contracts. We believe sunlight is the best disinfectant. We need to point a light on the government and show how inefficient and costly it is with certain services. At DPTM, we will then expose these enormous government costs and inefficiencies on media platforms, including social media.

Specifically, we will post cost comparisons of what it costs now with the government and what DPTM will charge for the same service.

Okay. Mr. Wonderful gets it. Like running TV ads and newspaper articles?

Yes. And radio spots and Facebook and Twitter and magazines, both paper and online.

Well, Sergeant Miller, I think you have an enormous mountain to climb, but Mr. Wonderful is here to assist. I will help you get on *Shark Tank*, but before—

Oh thank you, sir. Thank you. I will not disappoint you.

Yes, well okay. We'll see. But before I provide you pointers for appearing on the show, why don't we have ourselves another glass of that fine burgundy.

My advice is to target Mark Cuban.

Okay.

You know why, don't you?

I'm afraid I don't, sir.

Mark's very smart, and he's a bit political. You know I'm the only Shark who has dabbled in politics, right?

Really?

Absolutely. I made a run for prime minister of Canada, my home country. I ran as a Conservative. My campaign went well, but I calculated I didn't have enough support in the province of Quebec. Anyway, you don't have to be an elected official to affect political change. Your business success will come when you effectively target the right agencies for your superior and cheaper services. And I like your idea of getting the word out to the people—and how you can save the taxpayers some money.

Thank you.

Mark's really a libertarian. Who knows, maybe someday he'll run for high political office, like the presidency.

Okay.

As a libertarian, Mark believes in the mantra that the government that governs least is the government that governs best. So, I think he'll be intrigued by your cost-cutting, efficiency-gaining business idea.

Great.

Mark is a self-made billionaire, and I find him to be truly the most competitive of the Sharks.

Cool. Thank you for the tips, Mr. Wonderful.

And he's extremely well versed in technology matters, so I think your business, which is centered on data analytics and social media, may get him interested.

Awesome.

Now, Daymond John is an interesting study. Do you know that three of us Sharks are dyslexic?

No, I didn't know that.

Yes indeed. It's interesting that a fair number of very successful entrepreneurs are dyslexic. Daymond is one. Barbara Corcoran is also dyslexic.

Really?

Yes. And yours truly here, Mr. Wonderful, is also dyslexic.

No?

Yes. Mr. Wonderful always tells the truth. But I've always looked at dyslexia not as a setback, but as an asset. I overcame it, so I have the confidence to tackle obstacles in life and in business. It also makes me look at things from various perspectives.

I see.

Daymond is successful and self-made, like all of us Sharks. His strengths are fashion, production and logistics, and cultural trends. My gut tells me, though, that your business idea won't interest him. I might be wrong, but Mr. Wonderful's gut is often right.

Okay.

Now, Barbara, she made her fortune in New York City real estate, and she has a good eye for marketing and sales. She's done quite well in the food space too. And like me, she's dyslexic, or at least she was as a child.

Okay. I see.

I'm very analytical with my investments, but like I said earlier, I at times go with my gut. Barbara, in my experience, almost always goes with her gut.

Okay. Good to know.

With Barbara, she not only has to like your business idea; she has to like *you* as well. I think you're a likable fella, Sergeant Miller, but here's the thing: I'm quite certain Barbara is conflicted out because she's a spokesperson for Paycom. Grasshopper, Mr. Wonderful strongly advises you to tread carefully if you want to pitch your idea on *Shark Tank* because the no-nonsense truth is there's nothing proprietary about your business. Anyone can start a payroll and human resources company, and anyone can try to obtain government services contracts. If you're lucky, you'll get on the show, and if you're really lucky, Barbara won't be one of the Sharks that day. You know, we rotate; there's several of us Sharks.

Yes, I understand that, sir.

At the end of the day, Barbara is a savvy Sharkette. For all I know, she's conflicted out, but there's nothing stopping her from pitching your idea to one of her corporate sponsors. Paycom could try getting government contracts too.

That's true, Mr. Wonderful. But we have unique data analytics, and—

Paycom has data analytics too. They can throw plenty of resources at analytics.

But our uniqueness is the cost comparisons and social media angle. I'll be filing FOIA requests left and right. Once the taxpayers realize certain services can be better provided and for less money, they'll demand change and cost savings.

Again, grasshopper, there's nothing unique about your business idea. Barbara is a nice person, but niceness means nothing in business. Business is about money. She may turn around and advise Paycom to do what you have in mind.

Understood.

Now let me tell you about Lori Greiner.

Okay.

In my way of thinking, Mark Cuban and Lori Greiner are the only two Sharks who were born as entrepreneurs. Well, maybe Daymond too. These fine folks knew at an early age they wanted to work for themselves. Barbara had many jobs before she got into real estate. As for Mr. Wonderful, I wanted to be a photographer. Robert Herjavec also fell into entrepreneurship—he wasn't born with it. But Lori, she always worked for herself. And like Barbara, for her to invest in your business, she not only has to understand and like the business; she has to like the person behind the business. She'll let you know if your business idea is a hero or a zero. Lori's the QVC Queen, an expert in consumer products and marketing. I doubt she'll be interested in a business like yours that depends on reforming the government.

I see. Thank you, Mr. Wonderful.

You're welcome, grasshopper. Now, about Robert, he's an interesting guy. Great energy, a motivated fella, a happy fella. He loves his motor toys—cars, motorcycles, boats. He's well versed in all these areas. He's made his fortune in cybersecurity, and I think he might actually be your best bet as an investor given that there's so much demand for cybersecurity in the government, and

I think he may want to use your business idea as an integrated platform to promote his main business.

I see. That makes sense. Good to know, Mr. Wonderful.

Very well. Now I've mentioned the so-called traditional Sharks, but there are some other savvy investors who might be on the show should you be so lucky to get on the program.

Okay.

I don't know all the Sharks who have made guest appearances, but I know some of them. I highly recommend you find out who the Sharks will be if you get on the show.

Okay.

One guest Shark is the billionaire John Paul DeJoria, who, like Mark Cuban, really grinded it out and lived sparingly for many years before he made his fortune, in his case, selling Paul Mitchell hair products. John Paul was homeless for some time, lived in his car, and sold encyclopedias too. He knows the value of a buck, and, like Barbara, he not only has to like the product or service you're pitching; he also has to like you as a businessperson. I'm not sure if he'd invest in your proposed company, but it's possible.

Okay.

The entertainer Jeff Foxworthy has also made guest appearances on the show. I find him disciplined and straightforward. His strength is understanding rural and Middle America. I don't know his politics, but I suspect he'd favor anything to bring efficiency and cost savings to government programs.

Okay. Good to know.

Steve Tisch is also a guest Shark. He's smart, polished, and connected. I actually think he would be a good match for your proposed company.

Nice. I hope he's a Shark should I be lucky enough to be on the show.

Sara Blakely is another guest Shark. She's a self-made billionaire whose fortune derives from her apparel company, Spanx. Sara has a strong sales and product background. My guess is a company like yours won't interest her, but I might be mistaken.

I see.

And my thoughts on Bethany Frankel, another guest Shark, mirror those about Sara. Bethany is outgoing and energetic, and she's strong in creating brands. I don't see your company as brandable, Sergeant, so, with that, I'd be surprised if Bethany would invest in DPTM Corp.

Well, that's good to know.

Richard Branson has made some guest appearances on our show. Like Mark and Lori, he's a born entrepreneur. He's been around the block a few times, has great insights, and let me tell you, this British billionaire is a risk taker. My guess is he may very well invest in your idea.

Awesome.

Another guest Shark is Rohan Oza, the King of Brands. He's very strong in the beverage industry and also in the food space. Mr. Wonderful always tells the truth, and the truth is I seriously doubt Rohan would be a prospective investor.

Okay. Understood.

Ashton Kutcher is yet another guest Shark. Let me tell you, my friend, Ashton is smart and really understands numbers when it comes to investments. A famous actor, his fortune derives from investments in Uber and Airbnb. If you're pitching to Ashton, you better know your numbers. You should always know your numbers, but especially with Ashton.

Thanks for the tip, Mr. Wonderful.

You're welcome, grasshopper. Now another guest Shark is the great baseball player, Alex Rodriguez.

Yeah. I've seen him on the show a couple of times.

Alex, like many Sharks, truly knows the value of a dollar. He was one of the greatest players, and he invested his money well when he was getting all that money playing baseball. Most of his fortune is tied up in real estate, but Alex has a good eye for products with potential. I don't know his thoughts on services though, and, let's face it, Sergeant, you're proposed company is all about HR services. My thinking is Alex will pass on your company.

Okay. Understood.

Yet another possible Shark is the NBA Hall of Famer, Charles Barkley. Charles is a smart, practical, down-to-earth person and investor. I think he may like your idea and give you a chance.

Great. Cool.

With that, young man, my advice to you is to start your company with your brother and hustle for some business. I know your target audience is the government, but all companies need HR services, so you should target small and big companies alike, not just government agencies.

Okay.

Mr. Wonderful speaks the truth, and here's some more advice: you increase your chances of getting on *Shark Tank* exponentially if you have an existing business set up that has sales. Because what are sales? Answer: money. You as the entrepreneur making money for yourself, making money to pay your employees, making money for your investors who took a chance on you, and, with your business model, saving money for the taxpayers. Money, my friend. That's the measure of business success. Work hard, get some contracts, and make some money. That will augment your chances of getting on the show.

Thank you, sir. I'll take your advice for sure.

Not only take my advice, but execute, young man. Do it. Make it happen. Business is about executing. Sam Walton, the founder of Walmart, started with an idea and a store. At the time, Sears was an American icon, an institution. Who could beat Sears at retailing? Sears had all the advantages—the real estate, the products, and the ability to raise capital—but they failed to keep their eye on the ball, to innovate, and to always make the customer, and his or her needs, their number one priority. Sam Walton is really the force behind discounting—selling a lot of volume at the lowest possible prices. He, at first, stayed away from the expensive city markets—real estate is always more expensive in cities and the suburbs—and he focused on small towns. His idea caught on, and he became the most efficient operator. Sears is dead now. Game over. Now in retailing, you have Amazon as a giant, but let me tell you, Walmart is increasingly getting into online sales and home delivering. The point is, Sergeant Miller, become the efficient operator. Never rest on your laurels—and always make the customers' needs your number one priority.

Yes, sir.

Your challenge will be your strong competitors, and there's nothing proprietary about your business idea. Any payroll company can decide to go after government contracts. Your idea is unpatentable. I think your idea could work, but my concern is your competitors will decide to do the same—compete for government contracts—and at that point, any margins you may have will plummet. You've got a tall mountain to climb, Sergeant Miller. I'm not sure if I'll be there with you for that journey, but I'm pleased to have provided you with sound advice for increasing your chances on appearing on *Shark Tank*.

And I thank you for that, sir.

You're welcome, grasshopper. Now, before we're through here in Mr. Wonderful's Wonderland, being that you are a military man, I have a request.

Yes, sir. Anything. How can I help you?

A friend of mine, many, many years ago, in fact, many decades ago, told me some of the sayings he used in the navy. I met this buddy of mine in Malta, and I've since forgotten these sayings. They were very funny, and at times instructive. I would use them on occasion during business negotiations. I'm thinking there must be some expressions and sayings you've come across in the army. Care to share any with Mr. Wonderful?

I see. Well, let me think. Uh, I already told you the running joke in our unit is that the Defense Travel System is really the Do Not Travel System. Oh, I've got one. You've probably heard what the acronym SNAFU stands for, right?

I've heard the term, but Mr. Wonderful, despite his vast amount of wisdom, has forgotten the meaning of SNAFU.

Too easy, sir. SNAFU stands for situation normal, all fucked up. Our first sergeant often throws that term around.

Mr. Wonderful likes it.

Cool. And another military acronym that I hear on occasion is NSTR. We see it a lot on PowerPoint slides actually. Stands for nothing significant to report. Quite a few meetings are pointless, and so often, when the company commander or first sergeant asks us to go around the table to report our final comments, lots of the guys simply respond, "NSTR, sir."

I see. NSTR. I like it, grasshopper.

Oh, and related to the acronym SNAFU is the saying "ate up like a soup sandwich." You hear that one when things are really messed up. Our platoon leader once was disappointed with the armor room. A big order had come in, there were boxes strewn everywhere, and the place was messy. He came in yelling, "You all are ate up. You all are ate up like a soup sandwich."

Nice. Mr. Wonderful gets it. And likes it.

Let's see. What else? Well, another saying is in the form of a question. It goes like this: Is the juice worth the squeeze? I've heard that question in a few military meetings. Means is the result worth the effort?

Excellent. That's your best one yet.

And here's another one. When you want to tell someone that they really don't have a choice, you tell them, "This ain't no Burger King; you can't have it your way."

Funny, my friend. I think that's your best one now. By the way, Burger King is a solid company. Their menu has improved quite a bit in the last couple of years.

I agree. McDonald's is probably the stronger brand, but Burger King has definitely gotten better. So has Wendy's. But there's so much competition in that space.

You're learning, grasshopper. Lots of competition out there: the brands you've mentioned plus Carl's Jr., Checkers, Smashburger, Five Guys, Zinburger, Fat Burger, Shake Shack, Johnny Rockets, Sonic, and White Castle. And out on the West Coast, I'd say In-N-Out Burger is crushing it. If they expand eastward, they'll do just fine.

Absolutely sir. I tried them out once in San Antonio. Nice fast-food restaurant, that's for sure.

And Shake Shack is crushing it too. Great brand.

Agreed. They're great. And they serve beer, which is a plus.

Right you are, grasshopper. Alcohol definitely has great margins, but come to think of it, I think the best fast-food restaurant out there is Chick-Fil-A.

They sure are busy in Lubbock.

Mr. Wonderful is always right. And Sergeant Miller, I must say, I like the "this ain't no Burger King" saying. That one too will find its way into my repertoire.

Cool. I'm thinking if there are any other army sayings. Hmmn? Oh, well the last one that comes to mind is another acronym. It's SLICC. Stands for "self-licking ice-cream cone." I heard that one during a meeting led by a battalion commander. He was obviously disappointed and frustrated with the government bureaucracy that can affect the army. There were a lot of civilian government employees at the meeting, and this commander at one point looked at the highest-ranking civilian employee and said something like, "You civis. Y'all just a bunch of SLICCs. Self-licking ice-cream cones is what y'all are. You do very little and serve no purpose. Your purpose is just to come here and collect a government check and then later collect a government pension. Your purpose is just to continue to exist. Keep licking that ice-cream cone of yours. If I had my way, y'all would be out of a job."

Mr. Wonderful is intrigued. SLICCs. Mr. Wonderful likes it. You know, come to think of it, with my interest in politics, I strongly believe that the world will increasingly divide into SLICCS and Randians. The SLICCS, as you put it, simply exist to exist—they serve no purpose really, except to protect their turfs and their budgets. It's not all their fault, but they just find themselves in unproductive work. Then there will be what I call the Randians. Many are self-employed. I name them after Ayn Rand. Are you familiar with her?

A bit. The writer-philosopher. *Atlas Shrugged* and *The Fountainhead*. I didn't finish either book. They are not easy reads. But I know she's big on individualism and distrustful of government.

Right you are, grasshopper. I once had a conversation with Mark Cuban, and during our exchange, he revealed to me he was an Ayn Rand fan. Like I told you earlier, Mark Cuban may be the Shark who'll invest in your company if you're lucky enough to get on the show.

Okay. But back to how I see the future. With the advances in automation, robotics, and artificial intelligence, tremendous efficiencies will be brought to the marketplace. SLICCs will want to preserve their unproductive jobs, and the Randians, who are independent, will make the best of it; they'll find productive work, often by being self-employed.

I see.

And, Sergeant Miller, let Mr. Wonderful give you one last piece of advice. I understand that your proposed business is about bringing efficiency to government services, but with the explosion of technology and robotics, I tell you this, young man: the business to get into will be the entertainment business. As data analytics bring efficiencies to the consuming public, more and more people will have free time. I honestly can see the workweek going from five days to four days a week. With more free time, people will desire more entertainment. I can foresee—maybe twenty years from now—sports leagues featuring competing robots, and maybe some leagues pitting humans against robots. And the real excitement with robots will be when humans can control the robots. Imagine me owning a robot that is programmed to box, and then you have your robot that is also a boxer. Me and you go at it with our robots. I think such a scenario will occur, and there will be enormous opportunities in the gambling industry as tons of people will want to bet on which robot—Mr. Wonderful's Robot or Sergeant Miller's Robot—will win the boxing match. Or the tennis match. Or the heads-up poker tournament. Baseball, football, hockey, car racing, ice skating—you name it, they'll be robots who will master these sports. And tons of folks will bet on the outcomes.

GRINDING IT OUT

MY EYES WERE SLOWLY OPENING up. I was laying down, bright lights illuminating the place.

"The surgery went well, Sergeant. We're just wrapping it up."

I was in and out of a fog. Everything was quiet, and then I heard someone say, "Okay. We're done. Let him rest. He'll need a lot of physical therapy, but he'll be okay."

I fell asleep, and when I woke up, I was alone in a hospital room. That didn't last long though, and I was soon attended to by different medical staffers. My stay at the hospital—Landstuhl Regional Medical Center near Ramstein Air Base, Germany— would last for another forty-eight hours, then it was two months at Walter Reed Medical Center in our nation's capital for physical therapy and tons of paperwork to fill out for the Department of Veterans Affairs. I was honorably discharged in November 2020, and I was back home in Lubbock for the holidays.

I resumed law school at Texas Tech in January of 2021. I needed sixteen credits to obtain my joint JD-MBA degree in time for spring graduation. Mom and Dad were kind enough to let me live at home to keep my expenses down, and with the combination of the GI Bill and my VA disability, I only needed to take out five thousand dollars in student loans.

Then 2021 just blew by. A heavy load of courses (some online on account of the dreaded COVID-19 virus); then the graduation (yeah!); then two months of serious studying for the bar exam (yuk!); then the pressure cooker of the bar exam itself (major yuk!); then the equal pressure cooker of waiting for your bar exam results (more yuk!); then the huge relief of finding out I passed the bar exam (big-time yeah!). But the biggest yeah! of them all was my girlfriend, Amy, an MBA student at UTEP (University of Texas at El Paso), who said yes when I proposed to her.

DPTM was incorporated in Austin in the summer of 2021 with me as the chief executive officer, Bob as the chief operating officer, and Amy as the chief financial officer. Bob, who was living in Austin, got busy with his artificial intelligence and data analytics, and I started filing FOIA requests left and right out of Lubbock. Amy, still in El Paso, wrapped up her MBA and started organizing our billing, financial statements, and marketing packages. In September, we applied to have DPTM featured on *Shark Tank* as a start-up, and in December, we received notice that our request to appear on the show was turned down.

I moved to Austin in early 2022, and Amy moved in with me. We lived two miles from Bob's townhouse, which served as the headquarters of DPTM Corp. I owned 50 percent of DPTM, and Bob and Amy owned the other 50 percent equally. We were living lean. Amy and I had one vehicle (my 2010 Honda Accord, which I bought from Dad). We only ate takeout once a month (ramen noodles, mac n' cheese, and peanut butter sandwiches made up a big portion of our diet). And our entertainment budget was our monthly Netflix subscription fee, and once in a while, a visit to our favorite music venue in Austin, Friends on Sixth Street (no cover charge). Bob had his full-time job, and at night, he kept building the database searches. Amy's days consisted of Zoom meetings and phone conferences with government agencies, and I kept filing FOIA requests to obtain costs of services. To make ends meet, I was driving for Uber four or five nights a week.

The result of our tireless efforts was a $20,000 one-year consulting contract for the City of Austin planning board. In July of 2022, we had again applied to appear on *Shark Tank*, but we were denied once more.

And 2023 kicked off as a repeat of 2022: grinding it out, living lean, doing our best to grow DPTM. Our big break came in October when we received the wonderful news that *Shark Tank* had accepted our appearance on the popular show (we had applied again in July after receiving a $75,000 contract with the City of Houston).

While we kept hustling for business, Bob, Amy, and I kept practicing and refining our sales pitch for *Shark Tank*. We made sure we had all our facts down pat and knew our numbers backward and forward. EBITA, cost of goods sold, we had that down. Customer acquisition costs were problematic, but I knew how to explain that.

In November, we were informed the *Shark Tank* panel would consist of the "traditional" set: Mark Cuban, Daymond John, Barbara Corcoran, Mr. Wonderful Kevin O'Leary, Lori Greiner, and Robert Herjavec. Normally, there are five Sharks, but we were informed the show would start featuring six Sharks, starting with the show we were accepted on.

SHOWTIME

ON DECEMBER 2023, WE WERE in Culver City, California. The three of us—anxious, nervous, excited, butterflies in our stomachs—were standing at the back end of that long corridor leading to the Six Sharks. The introductory voice came on, and the doors to the corridor opened.

"Welcome to the *Shark Tank* where investors pit their own money to invest in a business or fight each other for a deal. First to enter the tank is a trio who started a company to bring cost savings to government agencies and the American taxpayers."

On cue, we walked down the corridor. As practiced, Amy spoke first.

Amy: Hello, Sharks. I'm Amy Miller.

Me: And I'm Bill Miller, Amy's husband.

Bob: And I'm Bob Miller, Bill's brother and Amy's brother-in-law.

Us in unison: And we're the founders of DPTM Corp.

Me: Sharks, are we taxpayers getting the right bang for our hard-earned money?

Us in unison: No.

Me: Teachers, cops, and firemen being laid off while government spending continues to grow. Public sector pension liabilities that we know will bust the federal and state coffers. Waste and red tape that are endless.

Amy: But we at DPTM have a solution.

Mr. Wonderful: Thank God; stop the madness.

Amy: Exactly. DPTM stands for Don't Pay Too Much.

Bob: Sharks, our company gets government contracts at the federal, state, and local level. We consistently save government agencies 50 percent of their costs. Specifically, we handle hiring, billing, travel, and payroll services for government agencies. We're seeking a $100,000 investment for 10 percent of our company. So, Sharks, who's ready to join us and save the taxpayers a lot of money?

Mark Cuban: So, your company is about draining the swamp.

Bob: Yes, that's correct.

Lori: Tell us about yourselves and how you guys came up with this business idea.

Me. Well, I was in the National Guard while in law school where I was pursuing a joint law and MBA degree.

Robert: Thank you for your service.

Mark: Yeah, Bill, thank you for your service.

Me: Sure. And it was while I was in the army that I noticed a lot of inefficiencies. There were problems with my pay, and my colleagues were also experiencing similar issues. It also took forever to book our travel orders. And that's when the light bulb went off, and I figured there must be a better way.

Mr. Wonderful: Stop the madness.

Me: Exactly. My brother, Bob, was working in AI, and my then girlfriend—now wife—was getting her MBA. I thought, *I can do better*. So, we formed DPTM Corp.

Mr. Wonderful: Okay. Got it. Now let's talk about what really matters—money. You're asking for $100,000 for 10 percent of your company. You're valuing your company at one million dollars. Tell me why you think your company is worth a million dollars. What are your sales?

Amy: So far, we have contracts worth $175,000.

Robert: That's it? One hundred seventy-five K?

Amy: Yes, but we're currently in negotiations with the City of Dallas for a $300,000 three-year contract. And we're consistently marketing our services. The City of New Orleans is also thinking of awarding us an annual contract that's renewable.

Robert: How many employees do you have?

Amy: It's us and two employees.

Damon: And how do you obtain these contracts?

Me: We send proposals to government agencies. The best way to describe what we do is the word *transparency*. We bring transparency to government costs. Because of our data analytics and Freedom of Information Act requests, we know how much it costs government agencies to provide certain services. We compare those costs with our costs. We then post these cost differences to various media outlets, including social media, Facebook, newspapers, blogs, and our website. Why should the taxpayers pay more for payroll and travel services?

Mark: Well, I'm a big believer in the notion that information is not only knowledge but power, right? You guys are just as good as the information you gather. I'm guessing these government agencies are holding some of the data close to the chest.

Me: That's true. I keep filing FOIA requests, Freedom of Information Act requests, and quite often, we don't hear back—or we don't receive the entire picture. But we're good about finding out government employee salaries, government building lease costs, and also equipment costs. Right now, we're about to hire a lawyer who specializes in FOIA litigation. I'm good at filing FOIA requests, but FOIA lawsuits aren't my forte.

Barbara: You know what I think? I think you three are nice, good, decent people. But you have an incredible mountain to climb. In my many years in business, particularly in real estate, you know what I discovered? That whenever you're dealing with the government, it's nothing but mountains of paperwork to fill out, endless red tape, and everything moving at a snail's pace. Also, I think politicians are good about signing the backs of checks, meaning they are good at paying themselves. But they don't know what it is to sign the front of checks, meaning paying their own employees because they don't have employees—and many of them have never started a business. All they ask for are budget increases, more money from us taxpayers. And I also have to reveal that I'm a spokesperson for Paycom, so I'm conflicted out. But with all of that, I wish you all good luck climbing that incredibly tall mountain.

Me: Thank you, Barbara.

Lori: I have to agree with Barbara. I'm really a product person, not so much a services person. I think you guys are doing well and hustling for business, but I don't know how I would be value added. With that, I'm out.

Bob: Thank you, Lori.

Damon: I too can't see how I could help you, so I'm also out.

Amy: Thank you, Damon.

Robert: I think what you guys have built is great. You've solved the problem of saving costs, but to Barbara's point, anything dealing with the government is messy, man. Have you guys tried to bring these cost savings to corporations as well?

Me: We're looking into it, but frankly, companies are pretty good at saving costs. A big cost savings for us is we do everything from home. Our two employees also work from home. We have great payroll software that we're always fine-tuning. COVID-19 brought the issue of less leasing of office space to the forefront. Companies have cut their leasing space tremendously, but government agencies have not. Once taxpayers find this out, they'll demand change.

Robert: Look guys, I applaud what you've done. I wish you good luck, but you guys have a tremendous journey ahead of you that includes litigation, and I won't be on that journey with you. I'm out.

Amy: Okay, thank you, Robert.

Mark: Okay, here's where I'm at. I've known folks who have done government contracting, and one thing you should know is the government favors minorities and disabled veterans. And also—

Me: On that point, Mark, you're absolutely right. I should have informed you all that I'm a disabled veteran. Injured in Afghanistan. When we bid for contracts, that fact is in our bid.

Mark: Okay, that's good to know. And sorry to hear about your injury. But Barbara is spot-on with the hurdles of dealing with government entities. Now I like the fact that you guys have carved a niche, and that you have the information to post cost comparisons, but when I really think about it, the hurdles you guys will have to go through are not business hurdles. They're political and legal ones. Let me tell you, many government employees are unionized, and the managers of these government agencies really have no incentive to reduce costs. So with that, I'm out.

Me: Mark, can I just say something on that?

Mark: Well, I'm out. It's not going to change my mind.

Me: Understood, but the core of our business success is to inform the taxpayers how much money they would be saving if our company was awarded a contract to provide the service. As you put it, there are no incentives to change government services, but now there is. The taxpayer will realize just how much these services cost. That's why taxpayers will pressure the government to go with a company like ours. That's why we named our company Don't Pay Too Much.

Mark: Bill, great sales pitch, but I'm still out. You're dealing with political stuff that will be messy, and I don't like a mess, nor do I invest in a mess.

Me: Understood. Mr. Wonderful?

Mr. Wonderful: Well, as is so often the case, all roads lead to Mr. Wonderful. Now, I believe I'm the only Shark who has run for political office.

Mark: Oh, here we go.

Mr. Wonderful: Silence, Mr. Cuban. I ran for prime minister of Canada knowing that politics is a brutal business, and my dear young entrepreneurs, you have no idea what you're getting into. Politics is difficult to change, my friends, and I don't see a bright future. I have a story for you all. A nephew of mine served in the armed forces, and one night, while we were sharing a bottle of Chateau Ausone-Saint Emilion Grand Cru—a very expensive bottle of wine I might add—

Barbara: Why does everything have to resort back to wine with you?

Mr. Wonderful: Silence, Ms. Corcoran. As I was explaining, while my nephew and I were sharing a wonderful bottle of the real good stuff, we got on the topic of expressions in the US Army. And I must say, I believe a few of these sayings are apropos for your business idea. One such saying is snafu. You may know it stands for "situation normal all f-ed up." Another one is "this is ate up like a soup sandwich." Now I like soup, and I like a sandwich, but I don't like a soup sandwich. Your business idea, folks, is a snafu and a soup sandwich. Personally, I don't know how you guys made the cut to appear on this show of ours. Your business involves an incredible amount of squeezing for so little juice. This ain't no Burger King—you guys can't have it your way. No way is your company worth a million dollars. Your valuation is not only off; it's way off. Please take your business idea behind the barn and kill it because it's a loser. You all should do something else with your lives. With that, I'm out, and with severe prejudice. And I highly recommend you all execute an about-face and exit this forum because your business sucks—and you are nothing to me.

Amy, Bob, and I were embarrassed. We left that portion of the studio without an investment from any Shark. At the end of the corridor, we were met by an attractive middle-aged blonde who stuck a microphone next to my mouth and asked, "How do you think it went in there?"

"Well, we weren't successful in getting an investment. We know we have a tough road ahead of us, but we're committed to our business, and we're committed to saving money for the taxpayers."

We left the *Shark Tank* studio, took an Uber ride (Uber was popular in those days), and we got dropped off at our hotel. We entered our room—the three of us shared a room to save money. Can you imagine we paid two hundred dollars a night back then? Now, a room like we had would easily go for ten times as much, something like two thousand dollars a night. Anyway, we got to our room, cracked open some beers, and ordered delivery pizza. That too was through Uber, Uber Eats actually, not like the drones we have today. And while we were munching on our pizza slices, I got a phone call.

A ring on my then Apple iPhone, not like the audiovisuals we have today. It was an unlisted number, and, back then, I couldn't see who was calling me. I answered, "Hello?"

On the other end I heard: Hi. This is Steve Ballmer. I'd like to speak to Bill Miller.

Speaking.

Well, Bill, I saw your business proposal tonight on *Shark Tank*. I saw that the Sharks weren't interested in investing in your company, but I've got to tell you, I'm interested.

Wow. That's great news, Mr. Ballmer.

Please, call me Steve.

Well, Steve, I'm aware of your past business success at Microsoft, and am aware that you're the owner of the LA Clippers. We'd love to get an investment from you and to have you as a partner.

That's music to my ears, Bill. It's exactly why I'm calling. You're probably not aware that back in 2007, I founded USAFacts, a nonprofit organization that makes government data more accessible and understandable to our citizens. We're about acquiring government data to drive fact-based discussions. Taxes, Medicare, energy costs, military budgets—you name it, we have data on it.

Wow. That's great.

Yes, it is. We're having a positive impact, and I'd love to invest in your company.

Oh, thank you.

And there's a couple more organizations I'd like your company to pair up with. One is Openthebooks.com, another nonprofit that's dedicated to bringing transparency to government. Their motto is "Every dime, online, in real time."

Cool.

And there's a Washington, DC-based nonprofit called Citizens Against Government Waste. I'm confident these nonprofits are great fits for your company.

REFLECTIONS

I OWE A HUGE DEBT to Steve Ballmer because he was such a great operator. Shortly after our failed pitch on *Shark Tank*, he gave us that awesome phone call and the great contacts of USAFacts, Openthebooks.com, Citizens Against Government Waste, and the Government Accountability Institute, which was founded by the late Peter Schweizer. These organizations all made our data collection, artificial intelligence, software applications, and FOIA requests much better and more refined. Our marketing efforts probably increased tenfold after that phone call, and we started getting more government contracts.

That's great, Bill. My guest today is none other than Bill Miller, the richest person on earth. And here we are, in Las Vegas, America's second largest city right behind the Big Apple, New York City. Bill, you're eighty-eight years old. What do you attribute your success to?

Well, Susan, I don't think there's one thing: there's no magic bullet. Like I said earlier, I owe a lot of thanks to Steve Ballmer of USAFacts, and Openthebooks.com, which was founded by Adam Andrzejewski. That was decades ago. When Bob, Amy, and I were starting out, Mr. Ballmer and Mr. Andrzejewski really showed us the ropes. Of course, I'm also indebted to Mark Zuckerberg for buying us out shortly after he bought out Palantir, and I also need to mention Peter Thiel. As you know, Peter cofounded Palantir, and he was instrumental in persuading Mark Zuckerberg to buy us out. Now, a short story about the buyout, if I may.

Yes, please, go ahead, Bill.

Well, when Mark bought us out, Amy, Bob, and I remained significant shareholders, and Mark let us keep running the company. We expanded our contract base from government agencies to corporations. We all made a lot of money with the buyout, and our share price at DPTM kept posting solid gains and increased valuations. With our windfall from the buyout, Bob, Amy, and I decided to diversify into other businesses, mainly entertainment.

I ended up buying Bob's and Amy's shares before their deaths. Bob, as you know, died young, at fifty, having never married. He was really the brains behind the operations with his skills in artificial intelligence and software. I wouldn't be here today if it weren't for him. And as you probably know, my dear wife, Amy, died a few years back. We have four kids, eight grandkids, and two great-grandkids. I bought her shares before she passed, so that's a specific answer to your question as to how I became the world's richest person. Then again, I forgot to mention our failed sales pitch on *Shark Tank*, which, after all these years, is still on the air. We were lucky to get on the show, but we didn't get any Sharks to invest in DPTM. However, the late, great Steve Ballmer saw the show, and he gave us a call informing us he wanted to be part of DPTM. Maybe there's credence to the saying that sometimes good things can come from failures.

Thank you, Bill. And when we come back from a message from one of our sponsors, we'll have more questions for the world's richest person.

Desiring fun and adventure? Tired of the quick, short visits to the moon? For a real lunar experience, book your next trip to the moon with Lunar Travel. Lunar Travel offers stays at our resort for a minimum of three days all the way up to a month. Enjoy golf, swimming, guided tours, and world-class cuisine at our secure lunar dome. Pets and robot friends are welcomed, free of charge. Reserve now to take full advantage of our various discounts—and book your next adventure with Lunar Travel.

And we're back. I'm Susan Bentz, and my guest today is none other than Bill Miller, one of the cofounders of DPTM Corp., and the world's richest person.

Now, Bill, is it fair to say that most of your wealth is in the entertainment business? You're a key reason why this great city of ours, Las Vegas, became the entertainment capital of the world. I enjoyed reading those sections in your book where you describe your big bets on Las Vegas.

Sure, well, with the windfall from the buyout from Facebook, we were left with the decision on what to do with all this money.

And how much money are we talking about?

It was right around two trillion dollars.

Okay.

And I just had a gut instinct—I don't know where it came from, maybe a dream or something—but I felt that robotics and artificial intelligence would continue to grow. And I foresaw that more and more work duties would be filled by robots and AI. With that, I just figured this would give us humans more free time to do more of the things we wanted to do, especially physical stuff. I'm a man, and I think like a man. I figured we can have all the self-driving vehicles in the world, but there will always be a segment of the population—both men and women—who want to drive cars, motorcycles, and boats and do physical stuff like working out at a gym, hunting, fishing, cooking, gardening, bicycling, and kayaking. Things like that. I persuaded Bob and Amy that we should invest in these industries, along with robotics and AI. And those investments paid off. We bought a lot of land

34

around Las Vegas and opened racetracks for cars and motorcycles. We sunk money into a large man-made lake, Lake Vegas, where we now have a lot of boating and fishing. Golf is huge, and so we built tons of golf courses, all around Vegas. And firing ranges are also popular, so we have a lot of firing ranges. We also sell a lot of guns for recreational shooting. Then the light bulb really went off, Susan. My thinking is gambling was always big and will continue to be big. So, we bet heavily on gambling, especially sports betting. We bought out some casinos and bet big on sports betting. I think sports betting accounts for 60 percent of my fortune.

Susan, the investment bet that really paid off was robotic sports where people can build their robots and have them compete against other robots that are also built by other folks. As you know, we have sports leagues for such robots. It's been huge and will only get bigger. We've had the Robot Olympics for twelve years now, and it has been a huge hit with the biggest viewership ratings ever. People want to see robots competing against other robots, whether its boxing or some other sport. Some of the robots are controlled by humans—those are very popular—but sometimes we have the non-human-controlled robots just competing on their own, making their own decisions without human intervention. As you probably know, Susan, the most popular sports—and the ones that generate the most sports betting—are our Man versus Bot, especially boxing, and poker and cooking competitions.

And speaking of Man versus Bot, will you be watching the Johnson versus Kratos boxing match this Saturday?

Absolutely. I might be old, but I still like to watch sports and bet on them.

And did you place a bet on this big fight, the Johnson fight?

Yes, I did. There'll be five fights on Saturday, and I placed bets on all of them. The Johnson-Kratos fight is the main event, of

course. My heart is with Johnson, but my mind—and my bet—
is with Kratos. Kratos was originally programmed by the great
Ukrainian engineer Danylo Melnyk. I don't bet against Melnyk.
He'll make his programming adjustments, but programmers like
him can't make any adjustments forty-eight hours before the
fight. The commission takes over the robot at that point to ensure
there's no hacking.

Bill, I must ask you, How much did you wager on the fight?

Combined, two billion—one billion US dollars and one
billion in Bitcoin. I made smaller bets on the preliminary fights,
and I've got a billion dollars betting that Kratos will beat Johnson.
The Kratos bet is in Bitcoin.

I see. And I remember reading in your book that most of
your sports betting has been on golf. You've made a ton of money
betting on golf.

Yes, that's true. When it comes to golf, the robot will always
beat the human. The vision, the force and accuracy of a swing,
the touch needed for effective putting, the calculation of distance,
the factoring of wind speeds—a robot will always beat a man or
woman at this game. When a bot goes up against a human in
golf, the robot wins 60 percent of the time. That's a 20 percent
spread, 60 versus 40 percent. I can make a lot of money with a
20 percent spread.

Now, what about a robot golfer versus another robot golfer?

Well, in those cases, I just get as much information as I can
about the robots and the golf course they're playing on. I've made
a bit of money there, but the odds are closer to fifty-fifty, so it
depends. There's hardly any variance—it's just chance. I also
factor who built and who's programming the robotic golfer. That
matters a lot to me.

By the way, your book is entitled *Luck and Pluck: How a Failed
Shark Tank Episode Made Me the World's Richest Person.*

That's correct. It's available exclusively on Amazon, still the world's biggest retailer and biggest publisher after all these years.

And how much does your book sell for?

One hundred fifty dollars. It's digital and audio all in one. The reader decides if they want to read it or listen to it, and they can keep switching back and forth to their liking. I insisted the book sell for less than two hundred dollars to ensure everyone can afford it.

Is your voice the audio voice, Bill?

Just the introductions. Amazon has gifted robots as readers. Great voices—and in any language.

Great. And I heard that all proceeds from the book will be donated to the cause of personalized medicine for all Americans.

Yes. I think every American deserves personalized medicine. Once we achieve that in America, then we need to export it to the rest of the world. Susan, it's quite simple: all our citizens deserve a medical chip implant that can alert them to any health care issues on the horizon. With my brother, Bob, we didn't catch his cancer soon enough. The data is clear: everyone with a medical chip expands his or her life span by five years, and their quality of life is much better too.

That's great, Bill. Thank you for sharing that with us. Now, in your book, you're also candid about your business failures. Can you share some of those with our viewers and listeners?

Sure. There were many failures. I plowed something like $150 million into pet robots. I thought a lot of folks would want a pet robot, be it a dog, cat, parrot, pig, whatever. We even developed a pet alligator. It was all a big flop. The fact is that people want live animals as pets. Maybe not a live alligator, but certainly a live traditional pet.

I see.

Another huge flop was vitamin meals. I thought the idea of just taking a vitamin in the morning for breakfast, one for lunch, and one for dinner was a great business idea. The vitamins did work, and consumers felt full after eating them, but the feeling of fullness didn't last too long, and it turns out that people actually like the taste and feel of food—definitely more than the bland taste of a vitamin. With vitamin meals, we ended up giving a lot of the excess to the World Health Organization and the Bill and Melinda Gates Foundation. We gave it away for nutritional purposes to the still developing world. It's sad, but it's true: there's still a lot of poverty out there and some malnutrition. Susan, did you know that a third of the world lives on less than forty American dollars a day?

Yes, I've read about the problem of world hunger and poverty.

It's awful. We need to turn it around. Technology is the answer, but the problem, in my view, is that not all governments and political leaders are pro-technology. Anyway, that's a different topic, but back to my business and investment failures. Another failure that comes to mind is space travel to the moon and to Mars. It's nice, fun, and a technological marvel that we can travel to these places, but such travel has not been profitable, especially considering the huge capital outlays we had to make to achieve these technological marvels. Also, there's a lot of competition in space travel. That's good for the consumer, but it's hard to make money in that space.

That's interesting, Bill. Now, switching gears, if I may. A lot of your book is devoted to the presidency of Mark Cuban. This goes back many years.

That's right. President Cuban was president for two terms, from 2028 to 2036.

You were a big supporter of his.

Absolutely. I still think he's the gold standard for American presidents. Right up there with Washington and Lincoln.

And why is that? Why were you such a big supporter of his back then?

Well, President Cuban, as a self-made tech billionaire, really understood technology and the productivity capabilities that come with technology. With him at the helm, we finally had a fact-driven, data-driven, and efficiency-driven president. President Cuban found ways to finally cut federal spending without hindering government services. He knew what needed to be public sector and what needed to be private sector. Under his leadership, the government got rid of the US Postal Service. Companies like FedEx and UPS and DHL and Amazon were great and are still great about delivering the mail. Delivering the mail is not something the government needs to do. The US Postal Service was losing money year in and year out. Their infrastructure was a mess, and their pension and health care obligations were bank busters. President Cuban found a way to honor all those pensions and health care costs, but, importantly, he privatized the postal service, and that was a great move. Back in 1992—this was before I was even born—another Texas billionaire, Ross Perot, was saying the US Postal Service should be privatized. Well, it took some time, but it was another Texas billionaire who got the job done. President Cuban also privatized the VA in the sense that our veterans can now go to the doctor of their choice. The VA now is like Medicare—a benefits program as far as money transfers go, but the VA no longer runs medical clinics or hires doctors. Back in the old days, the VA was just one big bureaucracy with a lot more bureaucrats than medical providers such as doctors and physician assistants. Also, I must say that President Cuban really understood privacy. He outlawed telemarketing, which was a big pain in the butt and an infringement on our privacy.

And what about taxes? That was in your book too?

Oh, yes. How can I forget? President Cuban is the only politician I can remember who really addressed the issue of our complicated tax code. He did a great job of simplifying the code, and once that happened, the United States started getting so much investment capital, not only from our citizens, but from foreigners. There's no doubt about it, Susan, we live in the greatest country every created. I should have mentioned that as the big reason why and how I became wealthy. The great Warren Buffett said that many years ago. He said he became wealthy because he won the lottery—he was born here in the United States. In that sense, we all won the lottery.

But back to President Cuban, I have to say that he was great at selecting talented people. President Cuban did a great job in selecting Peter Schweizer as the head of a new cabinet post, the Office of Government Accountability and Transparency. Secretary Schweizer and his great team did an awesome job at fixing government and reducing waste, fraud, and corruption. Adam Andrzejewski also deserves a lot of credit as he was the deputy of that great agency. Those two great Americans really understood that humans are corruptible, but robots aren't—at least if they're not programmed to be corrupt and to show favoritism. The federal government, and also the state governments, really became better run because of Mr. Schweizer, Mr. Andrzejewski, and President Cuban.

In my opinion, Susan, President Cuban was a transformative president. After his two terms, the Republican Party rebranded itself as the Populist Party, and the Democrats saw that they stood as the opposition, so they rebranded themselves as the Progressives. The discussion really was forced to change because of President Cuban. Because of President Cuban, nobody, whether Populist or Progressive, argues for the return of humans as umpires or referees in sporting events. President Cuban really understood where human judgment was needed and appropriate, and where machine learning or robots with AI are superior to human judgment. Police officers, lawyers, writers, journalists, judges, and jury members—though there are measures to allow robots to fill these roles—it was President Cuban who warned about such movements and made it clear that those important functions are best filled by humans with human judgment. But sports referees, hedge fund managers, long-haul truck drivers, some military positions, such as certain combat roles, are best done and accomplished by robots. Also, some medical surgeries are better accomplished by robots and their steady hands; you never know when your human doctor is under the influence of alcohol or drugs. With teachers, it's fifty-fifty. Certain skills are better taught by humans, but others are better taught by robots. The point is, President Cuban understood these issues. He changed America forever and for the better.

That's interesting, Bill. We need to take a quick commercial break, but when we return, I want to discuss why President Cuban brought an end to libraries.

Sure.

Ready to blow off some steam? Come visit Physical Heaven. We're located thirty-five miles outside of Las Vegas. Our most popular service is the Five-Hour-Fun-Load. One hour of car racing, followed by thirty minutes at a firing range, thirty minutes of playing video games, then an hour of hiking trails, an hour of cycling, and to wrap it all up, an hour of cooking your own meal. All for the low and affordable price of five thousand dollars. That equates to an hour of fun for one thousand dollars, multiplied by five. Reservations are mandatory. Oh, and if you want, you can compete against a robot in all of these activities. Check us out at Physical Heaven. Reserve your slot today at 1-800-Hea-vens.

We're back, and I'm with the richest person on earth, Bill Miller. Now, Bill, I know you were a big supporter of President Cuban. I wanted your thoughts on why he brought an end to libraries.

Well Susan, President Cuban didn't bring an end to libraries per se. We still have the Library of Congress, as we should, and states and local communities can still have libraries if they so desire. But President Cuban recognized that if someone has a computer with internet connectivity, then they effectively have a library at their fingertips. He simply pushed for everyone having a personal computer—what we now call an audiovisual or AV. There's really no need for brick-and-mortar buildings housing physical books. All books are digital now, and they have been for a long time. President Cuban provided federal funds to ensure everyone had a computer with internet connectivity. His administration looked at budgets, and local communities realized that large libraries housed in buildings cost a lot of money. Utilities, building maintenance—it gets expensive. Plus, hardly any folks were going to libraries anyway. It became a cost-efficient and budget issue.

And in your book, you make it clear that President Cuban became an investor in your first start-up, DPTM Corp.

That's correct. Not at first. Like I said earlier, we didn't get any of the Sharks on *Shark Tank* to invest in us. It was after Steve Ballmer and the great entrepreneur Peter Thiel that Mark Cuban became interested in DPTM. He was very gracious. He told us he wanted to make a million-dollar investment. That was, like, two years after we appeared on *Shark Tank*. I have a lot of respect for someone who doesn't sugarcoat things and look for excuses. Mark Cuban simply told us something like, "Upon reflection, I now see the greatness of your business idea, and I would like to be part of it." We were very fortunate to have him as an early investor.

That's an interesting story, Bill. I see one of our producers telling me we have to break for a message from one of our sponsors. We'll be right back.

Tired of the rat race that is life? Tired of having robots everywhere doing things you could do for yourself and your family? Tired of having no purpose and meaning? Search no further because we not only have the answer for you, but we live it. Join us, the Church of Win-Eau. We're an independent sovereign territory in Brazil with a growing membership from all over the world. We grow our own food (no more nasty-tasting vitamins), fish our own fish, slaughter our own livestock, farm our own land, build our own houses, make our own music, act in our own plays, and teach one another important skills like reading, writing, math, carpentry, and gardening. No more Robo-Teachers. Our name derives from the final three letters of the last names of the great Charles Darwin and Jean-Jacques Rousseau, two giants who really knew how we humans came about and how we should live. Contact us today for more information at 1-800-Win-Eau. Remember, you can change your life by changing the way you live. Let us help you make human friends and live life the way it was meant to be lived. Offer not available to cyborgs with greater than 10 percent machine parts.

And we're back. I'm Susan Bentz, and our guest today is Bill Miller, the world's richest person. Bill, we left off with a discussion about President Cuban who, after encouraging the closure of libraries, ensured everyone had an audiovisual with the internet.

That's right, Susan. Back then, the device was called a smartphone, but now we have audiovisuals. Back in those days, we actually had to type our texts instead of speaking them. Tech titans like Bill Gates and Mark Zuckerberg and Reid Hoffman and Steve Wozniak and Michael Dell all got on board and supported President Cuban's initiative. The real operator was

Sheryl Sandberg, who President Cuban appointed to ensure every American got an audiovisual and internet connectivity. Ms. Sandberg executed a great government program. Folks who couldn't afford the device and internet were given vouchers, and in three years, it was mission accomplished—everyone had a computer and was connected to the information highway. With that, everyone basically had a library at their fingertips.

I have to mention, Susan, that it was President Cuban who created the Office of Government Information, an agency fielded by robots who know just about everything and can speak their incredible knowledge in any language. OGI is the source for government information. Anyone can call them and speak to an incredibly competent robot. How do I file my taxes? How much did it cost the navy to build the USS *Biden*? How many metric tons of grain did the US export last year? Steve Ballmer's USAFacts and Adam Andrzejewski's OpenTheBooks were important catalysts for OGI. All FOIA requests are expertly handled by OGI. And it was President Cuban who mandated, by executive order, that all public information be posted on OGI within twenty-four hours of its appropriation, and it's mandatory to also post when the money is actually spent. The people have paid money—through taxes—to generate the information, so we, the people, own the information.

But what about privacy concerns, Bill? That's been such a hot button issue for many years now.

That's true, Susan. Listen, the CIA's budget is and should be classified, so that's not disclosable. And a lot of information is still redacted—as it should be—for the exact issue you raise, privacy concerns. For names of people, internal business practices, and things like that, the FOIA exemptions still apply. And since denied FOIA requests are often litigated, our courts decide what is and what isn't releasable. If the government posts it on OGI, it's available to the public. The government is here to serve us—not the other way around. President Kennedy may have been an inspirational speaker, but he got things wrong when he said, "Ask not what your country can do for you; ask what you can do for your country." Famous saying, but he was wrong. The government works for the people and not the other way around. What makes America great is people pursuing their best self-interests. Our privacy is important, and so is the government's privacy. President Carter was right to set up FISA courts. These courts screen information before it's posted on OGI.

Thanks, Bill. And when we return, I'll have more questions for the richest person on earth.

Tired of the challenging dating scene? Tired of personality differences, differences in interests, and not being on the same page? Don't despair because we have the answer. At Robo-Dating, you date a custom humanlike robot made just to your specifications. The looks, personality, interests, even the voice are all chosen by you and made to your specifications. And your love life? Well, don't get us started. For dating filled with great conversations and great times, choose Robo-Dating. Visit our site today at Robodating.com and get started on your new dating scene. Robots ship to your home in forty-eight hours.

And we're back with Bill Miller. I'm Susan Bentz, and this is *Talking with Susan*. Bill, in your memoir, *Pluck and Luck*, you call into question some creative ideas that may have cost too much. Can you discuss those?

Sure. Well, as you know, Susan, CrichtonLand was set up in Oregon ten years ago and cost a fortune to the taxpayers. It's a public-private partnership, but it's mostly funded with government taxes. It's a fifty-thousand-acre park that draws decent crowds but loses tons of money every year; 90 percent of the dinosaurs are birds, and they eat a ton and crap a lot too. Tremendous food and upkeep costs. Michael Crichton was a great novelist—one of the greatest in my opinion—and Steven Spielberg was the greatest filmmaker. Crichton's *Jurassic Park* was a huge hit, as was Spielberg's movie of the same name, but the whole experiment has cost tons of money, and we have to ask ourselves if the juice was worth the squeeze. I don't think so. There were better uses for those billions of dollars. I think the figure is actually one trillion. I wouldn't be critical of this if the park was completely privately funded, but it isn't, so I remain critical.

And you've been critical of the Mars colony?

Yes, for the same reason: too much government money. Elon Musk was a genius, and he set up the colony. Everything was fine with him at the helm. His handpicked successors were okay, but they grew the colony too fast. The government—with good intentions—tried to help, but it ended up pouring good money after bad.

In your book, you wrote that Elon Musk was the smartest person you ever met.

That's right. He was. Mark Zuckerberg was another one, but Musk was a true gifted genius. As far as smarts combined with vision combined with communication skills, hands down, I have to go with Mark Cuban. But for pure brain power, Musk is the smartest person I've ever met, and I've met some pretty smart ones.

Switching gears, Bill, in your book, you mention that immigration is in part what makes America great. Can you talk about that and how you think we can improve our immigration policy?

Well, speaking of immigration, I just raved about Elon Musk, and he was an immigrant. So was the great Peter Thiel, another genius. Silicon Valley was and still is the epicenter of all the great technologies that have enriched our lives—although I must say that Austin, Texas, is not far behind. Did you know, Susan, that one-third of all Silicon Valley start-ups were founded by immigrants?

I read that in your book, yes.

Here's the thing, Susan. World population has been flat since 2065, but in the United States, we still have population growth. And we know that our population growth is not because of our birth rate; it's because people from all over the world want to live here.

Basically, Susan, the answer to our immigration issue lies within us, the people. We, the people, the taxpayers, are in charge. In business, the customer is the king. Well, in politics, it should be the same—we, the taxpayers, are the kings. The government is supposed to work for us. So, as I explain in my book, the answer to the immigration debate is to put we, the citizens, in charge. That means every immigrant who comes to this country has to have a sponsor, be it a personal sponsor, a corporate sponsor, an organization sponsor, or a church sponsor. The sponsor is financially responsible for the immigrant until the immigrant is eligible for a green card or citizenship. And we should still have the foreign student visa program, but once a foreign student completes his or her education, they can stay here in the United States as long as they have a sponsor. And, importantly, for an American business to sponsor an immigrant, that business has to convincingly show that the job was offered to Americans and that there were no qualified takers.

Thanks, Bill. We have to break again for a couple of messages from two of our sponsors.

Don't like the way you sound? Hate that voice of yours? We at New Voice have the answer for you. Our patented lab-grown vocal cords are available to you in an easy two-hour operation by an expert medical robot with the steadiest of hands. We accept most insurance plans, and low monthly financing is also available. Call us today at 1-800-NEW-VOIC and start your journey on picking and installing the voice you want. Remember, at New Voice, you'll finally sound the way you want.

Hi. I'm Rob the Robot, and I can personally guarantee you the best Robo Coaches because I'm in charge of them. At Robo Coaches, we have specially designed robots that suit your needs and will help you achieve the skills you desire, be it cooking, woodworking, foreign languages, picking up a musical instrument, one-on-one poker lessons, magic tricks, how to drive a mini spaceship—you name it, we have a Robo Coach for you. And, for the affordable price of twenty thousand dollars, we'll ship your Robo Coach straight to your home. Call us today at 1-800-Rob-Coach and start learning with your personal robot coach.

We're back with my guest, Bill Miller. Bill, in your memoir, you devote a long chapter to the complex issue of inequality.

That's right.

Can you explain to our viewers what we should do about this issue? It seems inequality has been a key political issue for so long now.

Yes, that's true, Susan. Inequality has sadly been part of the American story for a long time. I'm old enough to remember important cultural shifts that took place decades ago, like the Me Too Movement and Black Lives Matter. Sexual harassment and discrimination against women used to be a big problem, and, unfortunately, it's still a problem today, but improvements have been made. By law, human resource departments of companies have to investigate these serious allegations, and the Inspector General offices of government agencies also have to investigate such allegations. Black Lives Matter was about questioning whether our criminal justice system and its sanctions were being applied equally to all groups of people. Solid reporting and investigative policies came out of that movement, so that too brought about positive change. In my book, I argue that we have good systems and regulations in place, so what's needed is constant oversight and review of those regulatory programs. I also point out that today, the overwhelming cause of our inequality is gambling. Gambling began to explode in the forties and fifties when robots started replacing humans in the workforce. With more free time, we humans started spending more of our time with our hobbies and interests, and for a lot of folks, gambling, especially sports betting, became more and more popular. Frankly, Susan, I don't think we can get rid of sports betting because there's too much demand for it. The key is to provide counseling for folks who truly have a gambling problem. In the end, it's a choice issue; it's a freedom issue. And people will do what they want to do. Society and government can't change that. As we discussed earlier, I myself gamble a fair amount, and I largely made my wealth by investing in entertainment companies like casinos and sports betting operations. I will also tell you, Susan, that there's plenty of things to do with one's free time that don't involve gambling. Travel, including space travel, walking, hiking, water sports, sports of all kinds, cooking, reading, furniture making, music—whatever, the list is endless. I don't care what anybody tells you, I firmly believe that, overall, a human teacher or coach is better than a robot teacher. And these companies that advertise and promote the idea that the best sex is with a robot are flat-out wrong. I can't speak from experience, but I've read studies that show sex with a robot just doesn't cut it. Anyway, my key point— and I mention this in the book—is that you don't have to gamble to get ahead in life. There are plenty of ways to make money in this economy without gambling on sports. And there are plenty of things to do with your time that will bring purpose and meaning to your life. Family and friends and health are really important. You don't have to gamble to get those.

Thanks, Bill. And to shift gears some more, your book briefly discusses the Russian invasion of Ukraine by using its large army of robots. Ukraine is still occupied by Russian robots. What can we do about this? What can we and other countries do?

Well, as explained in my book, I advocate for more sanctions against Russia. There's also been strong condemnation from the world community against Russia and its invasion. I don't buy into the Russian argument that they were operating in self-defense. The facts show otherwise. Maybe a cyberattack to break into the Russian robotic computer code is in order.

Yes, it's complicated stuff, that's for sure.

True. The United States needs to gather support and work toward ending the Russian occupation. Dialogue needs to happen. President Trump's foreign policy team is working toward such talks—I think the venue will be Switzerland. That's a step in the right direction. It's interesting that the president's grandfather, President Donald Trump, was always accused of colluding with the Russians. Who knows how he would have handled—or not handled—the Russian invasion? Now his grandson is the president. Dialogue is definitely needed.

Yes, indeed. Well, Bill, we're almost out of time, so I have to make it quick. Your thoughts on the current marriage debate?

Well, right now, we have court cases deciding whether a human can marry a pet and other court cases ruling on whether a human can marry a robot. Then there's the whole legal issue of who or what is a human with all the cyborgs we have. Some state legislatures allow such marriages, and other state legislatures have enacted laws against them. Like I mention in my book, I'm against such laws. I think marriage should only be between two humans. Back when I was a young man, I supported gay marriage and transgender rights, and I still support such rights, but marriage between a human and a nonhuman? I'm opposed to that.

You're opposed to marriage with cyborgs?

Well, for that one, it depends. As a society, we're gonna have to figure out when a human is no longer a human. We're doing so many body replacements that the line is definitely fuzzy. And let me emphasize, Susan, that I'm not talking about lab-grown organs and body parts; I'm talking about machine body parts.

But isn't that hard to define, Bill? The distinction is a tough one at times, is it not?

True. We'll have to figure that out too, but what I'm saying is we have to draw the line somewhere. I think human-pet and human-robot marriages should be illegal. They are illegal in most states, but they need to be illegal in all states.

Why?

Well, Susan, I'm a businessman, and I think like a businessman. I know that marriage is not all about procreation—though that can be part of it—and I also know that marriage is not all about companionship, though that's part of it too. I think that marriage comes with certain rights that play into government welfare benefits and inheritance rules. And I think that a lot of these movements for human-pet and human-robot marriages are just a way to get government welfare benefits. It's a money grab, and I'm opposed to it. I'm tired of my taxes paying for things that shouldn't be paid for with taxpayers' money.

We're almost out of time, Bill, so I'll make it quick. Your thoughts on China and India? Pundits we're saying this century might be theirs, especially China, but that doesn't seem to be the case.

Right, Susan. Like I wrote in the book, if you're looking to start a business or invest in a company, stay here in the United

States. Canada, Europe, and Australia are also pretty good, and Israel is a true all-star. But nothing beats us, the United States. Entrepreneurship, small or big business, investor relations, financial markets—all of these things work well here in the United States because of our highly developed legal system. At times, I think we have too much litigation, but the point is we honor contracts and the law. A big problem for China and India is that they are plagued with a lot of corruption. The way to move up in those societies is to rise up in the government ranks or pay off the bureaucrats. There are millionaires and billionaires in China and India, but they have to obey what the government tells them to do. Another problem is China and India have never treated their women fairly, which is a big drain on talent. In that same vein, Chinese and Indian couples favor boys, and they at times practice female infanticide. It's awful. Here in the United States, the abortion debate is largely settled because of advanced contraception devices and free pregnancy tests. With that, abortions here and in other developed countries are very rare. Also, in the book, I mention that world population flattened out in 2065, but we here in the United States continue to grow, and that's because of immigration. China faces serious demographic problems, and that's not easy to reverse. Politically, the US is the best place to invest, and I would place Israel in second place. Capitalism puts the consumer first, and authoritarian regimes put the government first. We need to continue to put the consumer first. And we also need to put the taxpayer first.

And you argue for digital sovereignty in your book.

Absolutely. Every commercial sale, every internet search, the user should be asked by the program: do you allow our software and AI to track your location and collect data on your purchase? It's a yes-or-no answer from the consumer. Some consumers are okay with such data collection, and some aren't. It's up to the consumer to decide. How fitting it is to have this conversation with you, Susan, exactly a century after the famous novel by Orwell warning about the dangers of Big Brother, the dangers of too much government. When you put the consumer and taxpayer first, you necessarily have a check on Big Brother. Again, government is supposed to ensure our rights—not infringe on them.

Lastly, Bill, your book mentions three important life lessons. One, learn by doing. Two, never stop learning, and therefore, never stop doing. And three, life is a journey, not a destination.

That's right. I believe that, Susan.

And your journey has been a successful one, Bill, and continues to be a successful one. And to think that your journey would probably have been significantly different if you and your wife and your brother had not appeared on *Shark Tank*.

That's true, Susan. We didn't get a Shark to invest, but Mark Cuban did invest in our company later. And we got great exposure on the show. Like I mentioned earlier, the late Steve Ballmer saw the show, gave us that phone call, and told us he'd take a chance on us.

And *Shark Tank* is still on the air after all these years.

Yes, it's been an incredible run. Though the show is a lot different now. You know, ten years ago, I was invited to be a Shark, and of course I said yes, and I had a blast. Now the show includes two robots as Sharks. They're super smart and savvy investors, which makes them savvy Sharks. I still think humans are better judges of human character, drive, ambition, and risk thinking. Robots have more computational power than us, which makes them excellent investors of big companies, but they're not such great judges of the future success of a business start-up.

Your book ends with your thoughts on Jeff Bezos, another great entrepreneur of decades ago.

Yes, he was a great businessman. Bezos was correct when he argued that we have to limit and control the building of autonomous weapons. He also was right to point out that we shouldn't have Robo Cops and Robo Judges. We can use robots to check out dangerous buildings and help us put out fires, things like that, but police officers and judges need to remain professions held by humans. Bezos also was against robots as jury members. We now have a few states that allow some robots as jury members; the argument is that robots are "purely analytical."

The last line from your book is a quote by Jeff Bezos: "We are so unimaginative about what the future jobs are going to look like and what they are going to be."

That's right. I think Bezos said that in 2020. He was right then, and he's still right to this day. I think our best years are still ahead of us.

And with that, I thank you, Bill, for taking the time to discuss these important matters with us. The book is *Pluck and Luck: How a Failed* Shark Tank *Episode Made Me the World's Richest Person*. My guest has been Bill Miller. This is Susan Bentz. I'll be talking to you next week when our guest will be the world's oldest cyborg, Cyborg Willie.

Printed in the United States
by Baker & Taylor Publisher Services